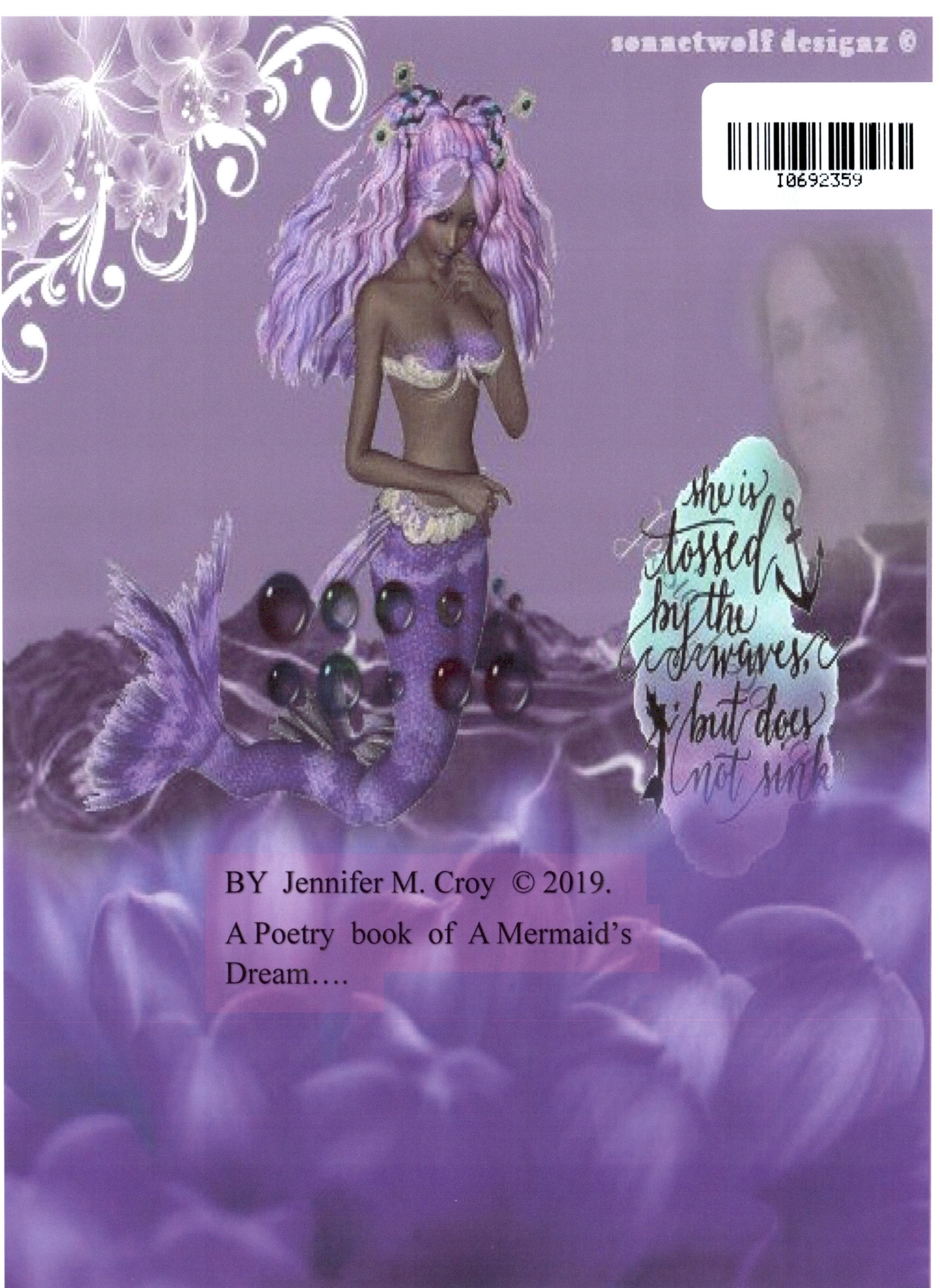

sonnetwolf designz ©

I0692359

she is
tossed
by the
waves,
but does
not sink

BY Jennifer M. Croy © 2019.

A Poetry book of A Mermaid's
Dream….

Dedication

to my family & friends who always believed in me to soar high like a shiny bright star in the sky. & Susan Joyner Stumpf my beautiful friend did the cover art work.

My husband Jim Croy who loves the poetic words spoke from my heart.

Find me on Facebook.com/jennifercroy.18

Goodreads.com email: jcroy20@yahoo.com

Amazon.com/jennifercroy's books

Lulu.com/spotlight/jennybooboo

Jennifer Book Store on Facebook.com

Barnes & Nobles. Com

Books a Millions website to order online

TABLE OF CONTENTS

She lives at the bottom of the ocean

Her siren captures the ships as they go by

Swishing her scaly tail high on a rock

Green eyes and brown hair sequined in a bubbly shell

She combs her long brown hair with a fork she has found

Treasures and trinkets of plenty

A thing of a bob I have many

Foaming waves fill the blue sea

Fishes and other creatures swam along side me

Pirates come to shore try to net the mermaid

She sped up fast and jumps high with the dolphins

Grabs on tight hold to the dolphins fin

And hurries below to her castle below

Enchantment at the bottom of the ocean

A bright colored castle lair with flair

King Neptune and merfolk live there

High on his throne where they all bow down to

Gold crown hovers on his head

And the mermaids sing melody songs

As he weds all his daughters of the sea

Protector, powerful king under the sea

Sees all his merfolk are not captured by fishermen above

Showers his people with safe, freedom of love

Mermaids of different colored hair pink, blue, brown

Plays a harp that they share

As all the creatures gather in dance around

Enchantment at the bottom of the sea

A Castle filled with Dreams

Mermaids swish their tails about

Below the sea surrounds the castle filled with dreams

Where the golden mermaid lair glistens in seaweed

Winding staircase rises up casting a glow

Bubbles float above as the water swishes below

Stormy sea thunders in the current air

As the merfolk take cover below hiding in the sand

She sings from the ocean depths

Planted on a rock above

She calls to the sea like an angel's love

Echoes throughout the land as her voice cries out

Bring forth the ships and fishermen lair

Flips her long brown hair

The seagulls, fishes, and dolphins hear her siren

She is admired from the sea below

That carries her melodious song of joy

The merfolk clap with anticipation

And wallow with admiration

A proud king of Neptune shouts

A booming sound below for all to watch and see

His daughter enchanted song sings out to thee

Pearls, Seahorses, and Echo Shells

Pearls in clams a treasure below

Seahorses swimming beneath the sea

Scaly fins rough and bumpy glowing brightly under the sea

Dancing, gliding, floating through the rolling waves

Shifting through the green seaweed forest

Hiding in the coral

Slowly drifting to the surface

Covered in white-frosted like patterns

A constellation of seahorses

The tide recedes, but leaves behind

Bright seashells onto the sand

Yet echoes in sweet, music refrains

Of the ocean calling out to me

A Mermaid's dream

Captured by the siren call

Of a mermaid's enchanted song

Fills the sea of creatures and fishes everywhere

Her swirly tail of blue calls out to you

Come forth and listen to a mermaid's dream

Swimming below the enchanted sea

Above the Ships Pass By

A serenade call as ships pass by

Snatching a fisher net to capture a mermaid beauty

A kiss can't compare to a mermaid's lips

A rare treasure to adore her merfolk girl fish

Who swims at the bottom of the blue sea

Enchanted castle playing a tune with a harp

A gale of stormy winds ride the current waves

King Neptune's powerful hand

Swirls the sea in the waters of the sand

Protects his daughters down below

From the fishermen cast above with a blow

The moon is set under a clear blue night sky

As the ships pass with one last try

The Calm Seas, Blue Waters

The roaring rippling waves

Foaming salt air in the breeze

Calm seas, blue waters

Hot sand bare feet curled beneath my toes

Moist, wet touch gritty particles felt

Melt lapping up of warm blue waters

Sun sets hover the horizon with a

Translucent moon beams down glistens

Twinkling stars a zillion light up the night sky

Jellyfish vibrant colors sway rays in the water

Have tentacles that sting small and big thing

Their mushy and gooey make you ill

Their stingers hurt and don't feel well

Mermaid sitting on a rock looking out at the Sea

She is tossed in the waves but doesn't sink

She calls out to her seashell pursed to her lips

The creatures come follow and dolphins jump

Sits upon her rock bubbles released around

Seaweed swaying below the rock

Fishes and a seahorse listen to her call

perched on her rock friends love thee

Neptune and Swim With the Dolphins

The tritons dancing in a ring

His palace and lovely daughters sing

he water with the echoes quake

Like the great thunder sound it makes

The sea-nymphs chant in accents shrills

Even the dolphins join in splash in the waves

King Neptune with his mighty pitch fork wand

Grasped in his hand rides the dolphin of the sea

Splashing, roaring in the choppy waves

Bow to all this mighty, powerful king of the land

Protector, harmonious strength gliding along

The sea with his white horses parading in victory

All The Fishes Follow Her

She explores treasure chest

Beyond all measures, trinkets and such

All the fishes follow her and love her as much

Starfish wishes of a mermaid under the sea below

Enamored with shells and be able to walk with legs

But alas she's a fish in water with a scaly tail

So free with king Neptune and his queen live

beneath the ocean shed their grace and love under

The magical ocean unseen by humans above

A prince to come save the mermaid beauty

And sail away as his queen

Bubbles In The Waves Of a Blue Lagoon

A blue lagoon like a pool

Bubbles dancing under in the light of the moon

Aqua-blue rays glisten in the night croon

Moonlight beams transforms the colored hues

Mermaid sings on a rock and swishes her tail

Strokes her fingers through her long, blond hair

The universe beyond compare

The white seagulls soar high above the sky

Listening to her lovely tune

They swoon and sway with other sea-creatures

Joyfully harmony in the enchanted waters

She Swishes Her Scaly Tail

She plays on a coral red reef bay

Swishing her scaled tail still

Or wriggling through the currents depths of the ocean

Swimming below to her green kelp palace

Laying upon a starfish bed

Seashells dancing in her head

Cold bubbles tickling her seashell bodice

Overflowing foam spills into my chest

Laughter shimmering bodies in spirals dance

Under the florescent lights beneath the sea

Whirlpool forms in the surface

She rides the Dolphin emanated in the blue Sea

The mermaid took hold of his fin roped around his body

Tugged on the reins and swam the blue ocean

mesmerized by every turn and jumping high

her friend the dolphin soaring above the tide

Swishing her long, colored scaled tail

Singing out to the sea, a tear she does not shed

Starfish wishes and fantasy enchanted spells

I listened to the sloshing of the waves against the rocks

Seahorses guided by King Neptune's mighty reins

As merfolk's greeted and bowed to their king

The daughters and queen mother wave at the king

Illuminated colors spun around blue, pink, and gold

Purple halo around the pale skin fair of the daughter's below

White sea shells and pearls of treasure added to the sea

Enchanted blue waters tame the calm stormy sea

Foamy bubbles ride the tide to the sandy shore

Upon the seaweed reefs at coral bay

True Friends Always Remain
In Each Other's Hearts

A friend is someone who listens to you without judging
Right or wrong, good or bad.
When you're feeling low about yourself
They gently help you to see the right perspective again.
A friend reminds you of all the positive qualities
You forgot you had.

When you share with a friend
Decisions are easier to make and problems seem less serious.
A friend gives you the precious gift of time
To talk about new ideas and desires
Of reaching goals and accomplishing dreams.
A friend loves you for who you are not what you do.
Feeling so accepted makes you want to try harder
And set higher goals
And accomplish more.

Through close friendship you learn the fine art of giving.
You begin to care more deeply and enjoy sharing.
Seeing the happiness you bring to another person
Increases your ability to love.
Wherever you may go in life a friend will always be with you.

Once in a Lifetime

You meet someone wonderful
Once in a lifetime

Once in a lifetime
Your dreams all come true

And life from then on
Can be nothing but special

My Once in a Lifetime is you!

Magical these creatures thought to be

Ever living in the sea

Rumoured to lure the unwary sailor

Mythical singer, banshee wailer

Amongst the rocks, in foaming waves

In and out of deep sea caves

Dreamy nights in watery graves

it's so cold without you here.
why can you not see i need you?
i need your warmth,
i need the love you gave...
the waters are so dark,
so lonely, without your light.

you sail away,
disappearing before my eyes.
do you even look back for me?
can you see me, bobbing alone,
under the light of the full moon?

i cannot see you anymore,
only the sails of the cursed ship.
that which carries you away,
carries all that is my heart.

i feel so empty,
my heart ripped from my chest...
the rain merely mirroring
my salty tears.

how could they not see
that i loved you?
that i alone cared for you?
how could you let them
tear us apart?

my heart shatters,
knowing within my soul,
you will never return,
if i let you leave now.

i sing out to you,
on the horizen,
my song begging you,
do not leave me...

23

She bobs her head above the water

Waiting for her sailor to come ashore

Can't you see me, my love?

It's so cold here, I need you

You sail away, leaving my tears falling

I need your warmth, your arms around me

Under the light of the moon, I call to you

I sing for you to embrace our love

But you disappear into the blue sea

Sailing away....

My salty tears long for your kiss

As I miss your strong, rugged face

Oh, how could you leave me, like this?

I swim back under splashing my tail

Hovered over in a fetal position, mourning you gone

MERMAID WALK

THERE WAS ONCE A FASHION PARADE OF MERMAIDS

LOOKING STUNNING IN THEIR CURLS

SHORT HAIR, LONG STRANDS, MANY WERE DRESSED IN PEARLS

THESE BEAUTIES OF THE SEA

THEY LOVED TO SWIM AND TALK

TO CELEBRATE "ART IN PUBLIC PLACES"

THEY CREATED THE MERMAID WALK

If I were a mermaid, and you were a sailor,
I'd follow your ship and lull you to sleep with my maiden songs.
I'd make the ocean rock you back and forth like a cradle.

If I were a mermaid, I'd wear dresses made of seaweed
and oceanfoam, dazzling blues and greens in the light.
You would think I was beautiful. Your eyes would be the color
of the ocean water, ebbing and flowing after the storm.

We'd dance to the sound of the waves making music and
the gulls singing swansongs, love songs played out in conch
shells over and over again. We'd clap clam shells together
and tap the bones of small birds on stones as drums.

If I were a mermaid, I'd give up the sea just for you.
I would learn to walk on rocky legs and climb aboard your ship,
where you would rock me to sleep in your arms.

Poetry My Inner Soul

Jennifer Croy

Sorrows & Blues

Jennifer Mary Croy

Biography:

I have written books of many since the 7th grade and working on several of my poetry books. I write to make me feel good inside deep soul of poetic words that I find sooths the person's body and soul. When we go through struggles or sadness, or even feeling hopeless Poetry eases the mind of writing about happiness of life. I have poetic friends who write about how they feel deep Inside of what they had endured as a child or went through in their lifetime. I also read poetry from some brilliant writers like Keats, Elizabeth Barrett Browning. I write to make me feel like a better person who has lived In the dark for a long time. But also to feel good about Myself that I accomplished writing poetry to make others feel better too.

sonnetwolf designz ©

she is tossed by the waves, but does not sink

www.ingramcontent.com/pod-product-compliance
Lightning Source LLC
Chambersburg PA
CBHW041542240626
47164CB00002B/100